Light Created the World
Persian Myths in Simple Language

Nana Valajam

• • •

Dedicated to the lovers of the world of myths

. . .

AURA ART GROUP

©Nazanin Nana Valajam 2024

auragroup2009@gmail.com

Edited by Michelle Goering
Book Cover Design by Maryam Ghoreyshi

ISBN: 978-1-7380250-0-8
ISBN: 978-1-7380250-1-5 (pb)

Printed in Canada 2024

• • •

Contents

• • •

Preface

Dear Reader,

The ancient culture of Iran—Persian culture—is disappearing. My sole motivation for writing this book is to preserve the myths and stories of Persian culture for the children and youth of Iran. These stories, from the Zoroastrian religion which is so central to Persian culture, and from pre-Zoroastrian times, are on the verge of being forgotten, and much of the culture with them. Preserving our history and culture is a task we all undoubtedly wish to undertake for our countries of origin: to protect the roots of our motherland for future generations.

There are challenges to remembering and passing along the stories. One is the difference in the language and written script of the sources of ancient mythological narratives from today's. These language barriers make original sources impossible for ordinary readers to understand.

Another challenge is understanding contemporary Persian literature and the tastes of the new generation, to tell the tales in a way that resonates for them. In this book, I have chosen simple language for storytelling and I have mentioned the references for those who are interested in learning more about ancient Persian stories and culture.

In addition to these translation challenges, the Iranian government does not deem the telling of pre-Islamic myths and research about them permissible; they are seen as a threat to the country's official religion.

Therefore, I decided to publish my research and collection of Persian stories outside of Iran, from my current home of Canada. They are not just for Persian children, but for all the children of the earth, and also for all adults who like the world of myths.

I believe that we humans, regardless of race, nationality, or generation, share a common spirit that binds us together, and understanding myths contributes to a deeper understanding of this collective spirit.

Hoping for peace in the world,

Nana Valajam

1. Creation in the World of Light[1]

In ancient times, when humans did not yet exist to live on earth, when in fact there was no earth for anyone to walk on, there was only Light and Darkness.

Light[2], alone in his world, sat high above, illuminating his world with knowledge and awareness. Darkness[3], alone in his dark world, sat far below, without knowledge or even a hint of thought to illuminate him! This is because wisdom, like the sun, like fire, was luminous, while ignorance, like absolute evil, brought darkness wherever it stepped.[4]

One day, Light decided to create endless joy and spread the light of wisdom throughout the world with this endless joy, which was a sign of a wise world. As soon as Light thought of endless joy, the world above became brighter.[5]

Darkness looked up from the depths below to the heights above and was amazed at the strange and wonderful works of Light and the smile he had on his face![6]

As Darkness was curiously observing Light, he realized that Light was making the luminous world more luminous. Suddenly, Darkness muttered under his breath: "More light! This is very bad!"

Yes! Darkness did not want the world of Light to become more luminous. He was afraid that amidst all this light, there would be no place left for himself, and eventually, Darkness would disappear forever.

*

While Darkness was looking up and lost in thought, Light brought forth endless joy in the form of seven beautiful angels. He gave each of them a special ability to attend to tasks alongside himself.[7]

Light turned to the seven angels and said: "I have created you from the essence of wisdom and goodness so that you may always remain alive and vibrant!"

The angels[8] looked at each other; they were delicate but strong, pure but brave, and intelligent for performing important tasks.

They looked at each other and enjoyed their endless beauty. It was time for Light to share a great secret with them. So, He stood near the seven angels and said: "I want to create a joyful world! A world that is full of beauty everywhere. You know, beautiful angels, joy needs care. And I want you to take care of the beauties and joys of the world.

Now watch carefully, because I want to bring forth endless joy in the form of sky, earth, water, fire, plant, animal, and human and show you how to take care of them!"

Those amazing angels, hearing these names, could see the glory of the sky, the beauty of the earth, the gentleness of the water, the brightness of the fire, the freshness of the plant, the goodness of the human, and the benefit of the animal, in their minds.

And with the imagination of this beautiful world, their existence was filled with smiles and joy.

*

Light looked at the row of angels and stood in front of the first angel, who was dressed in white and with eyes the color of the blue sky. Light named him Bahman[9] and said: "Handsome Bahman! You are the owner of superior behavior and thought. I want you to be able to distinguish all good thoughts from bad thoughts with your magical power and take care of beautiful thoughts and good ideas."

Bahman's blue eyes sparkled with joy. Light continued: "Remember that you also need to take care of animals, lest humans be able to harm animals on earth!" Bahman nodded in agreement and Light went to the second angel.

The second angel was dressed in yellow silk and her curly hair covered her forehead. Light took her hand and called her Ardibehesht[10]: "Beautiful Ardibehesht! You are the organizer of the whole world and you must remember that the law of the world is the law of pure ethics and good behavior. You must be aware that all humans should live happily together. The more people love each other, the happier they will be!" Light put his hand on her shoulder and continued: "Also remember that you need to take care of the fire– a fire whose flames dance and do not allow darkness to rule our world."

Ardibehesht, upon receiving this great responsibility, spun with such joy that her yellow skirt danced and shone like flames of fire.

The third angel stepped forward with firm steps. He wore a golden crown and had iron shoes on his feet. He had a silver belt around his waist and a copper ring on his finger. Light said: "I name you Shahrivar[11] and grant you the power of kingship over the earth. You must carefully and sensitively select righteous kings for the earth, because they are to make important decisions for humans.

In addition to this task, you will also be responsible for taking care of all metals. Do you know why? Because humans need metals for happiness. They must be able to make agricultural tools for themselves. They must plant many plants and have enough food. Because the day will come when their number will be very large."

It was the fourth angel's turn. She was a tall and wheat-colored lady. Her hair fell to her shoulders and she wore a red-gold crown on her head. White flowers bloomed on her dress and kindness flowed in her gaze. Light named her Spandarmaz[12] and entrusted her with the care of the earth. Spandarmaz had to take care of crops and fields, and support selfless creatures to achieve their goals. She had to make humans understand the real value of humility and selflessness so that their hearts would always have a place for loving others.

The fifth angel touched her own blue dress and straightened her silver belt. Light put his hand on the angel's heart and said: "The path of your heart is the path of all victories and ultimate happiness in the world. You can teach everyone the path of victory and perfection. Remember that you must take care of the path of rivers and running waters. You must be careful that these paths remain clean and free from pollution, because all living creatures need clean water." Then Light named her Khordad[13].

The sixth angel was standing next to Khordad. She moved a little to attract Light's attention. Light looked at the sixth angel, who had wooden shoes and was dressed in a soft velvet green dress, the same color as her eyes. The angel now took a step forward as Light called her name:

"Amordad[14]! I name you Amordad and entrust you with the responsibility of taking care of plants.

Amordad! From today onwards, you can teach humans that a right path is enough to become immortal and they should not look for other ways. They should never go towards competition and war. Competition and war destroy their happiness and you must remind them of this!" Amordad raised her head and with her beautiful eyes, confirmed Light's words.

It was time to name the seventh angel. Light named him The King of Wisdom[15], because he was made of complete knowledge. The King of Wisdom was so luminous that one could not look directly at him. Even the other angels had their tongues tied in admiration of his beauty.

Light entrusted the seventh angel with the care of knowledge to make a clear path from each sign of thought.[16]

*

Finally, the naming of the angels came to an end[17]. Throughout this time, Darkness had not taken its eyes off the world of Light for a moment. He trembled with envy at all this beauty. He had to do something to soothe his upset. And what else could he do but create filthy demons from that endless dark world within him to go to war with the angels of Light.

*

Darkness wove his dark thoughts and envy together to create seven demons from pure darkness to stand against the seven angels of Light.

The first demon created, Akouman, was filled with vile and chaotic thoughts, to stand face to face with the lofty and pure thoughts of Angel Bahman.

Then Darkness gave the second demon, Indra, such a disorderly form that it could disrupt the order of Ardibehesht's world. It didn't take long for Darkness to start creating the third and fourth demons.

The third demon, Savool, was made to disrupt the truths and destroy the worthiness of the people. Darkness whispered in its ear, stirring enmity, making it the foe of the angel Shahrivar.

Then from his filth, Darkness created Naghis, a demon to increase greed and envy so that no one would have any interest in sacrifice and everyone would be on the path of malice. Darkness looked at the demon of greed and envy with satisfaction and the first smile sat on his lips.

So, what could be more terrifying than the people contaminated with malice in the Light world? This fourth demon was the best rival for angel Spandarmaz and had the power to destroy the whole world in its being!

Darkness—this time with a darker heart—gave shape to the fifth demon, Teriz, and prepared it for enmity with angel Khordad, to prevent humans from reaching their desires and wishes.

Darkness thought: "Now only one task remains! Destruction! Destruction of the creations of Light!" And he created the sixth demon, Zariz, and gave it a deadly poison to come to kill and confront the force of life on earth. The sixth demon had to confront Amordad to be able to kill the creatures.

Darkness looked at the luminous world above his head. He saw that the seventh angel was the beauty of Light! This angel was so beautiful and luminous that Darkness could not stare at it! Therefore, he took a mirror in front of his face and from his ugliness and anger created a reflection named Ignorance or Ahriman—a demon that closes the doors of thought in every mind.

● ● ●

Darkness took such pleasure in the seventh demon that for a few moments he forgot why he had created it. Then he embraced Ahriman and ordered him to go to war. Because when anger increases in human thought intellect and knowledge fail, and that is when other demons can get to work and turn the world of Light into absolute Darkness.[18]

*

The task of shaping the demons was completed, and finally the world of Darkness had demons that could darken the world of Light and destroy endless joy. With optimism, Darkness put the demons on the edge of his world so that Light from high above could see them well.

Light looked at the world under his feet and laughed at seeing those ugly demons. He said: "How do they endure without joy? I must create more joys in the world against these strange demons. I will make small joys that support endless joy so that the cycle of joy does not fall." Then Light looked at the angels: "Come here! I want to give knowledge and wisdom to everyone so that all creatures can create more joys with their knowledge and choice."[19]

*

Light went to work again. He placed endless joy in the middle of the world and nurtured it well. The angels stood all around the endless joy and carefully watched the rest of the world being created.

Light took a piece of endless joy and made it look like flames of fire. Then he blew on it and the Fire of Wisdom[20] flared up—a fire whose flames were knowledge, purity, and morality.

Light shaped and enlarged the Fire of Wisdom to resemble a human—with a head and neck, a body, two arms, and two legs. The angels approached the Fire of Wisdom and circled around it to figure out what Light was doing.

The Fire of Wisdom was not at all like the fires that today burn and destroy everything with their heat. Rather, it was one of those fires that neither burn, nor smoke, nor leave any ashes behind. The Fire of Wisdom was truly a special fire!

Light waited a bit. The angels became restless from Light's silence: "Wasn't the plan to create the sky and the earth? So why did you create another angel?" And Light replied: "But this is not an angel!

This is the Fire of Wisdom and it contains all the world we need. Be patient. I want to bring the whole world into existence from this fire so that Darkness and the demons can not win over any of the creatures of our world! Do you know why they can't? Because Darkness can not find a way to light. And the light that never goes out is wisdom."

*

Light got busy again. He plunged his hand directly into the heart of endless joy, took a piece of it, and nurtured it well. This time he created the seasons of the year[21], just like the spring, summer, autumn, and beautiful winter that we know today!

He divided each season into three parts and separated the months. Again, he divided each of the months into four parts and created weeks. Then in the same way he created days, hours, minutes, seconds, and even moments.[22]

Light slowly breathed his breath into the pieces and time took on meaning in the world.

The angels lost their patience again: "What are you doing? Tell us, too!"

A smile formed on the corner of Light's lips: "I have to determine a time to bring each part of the world into existence. Time is very important. The day will come when people synchronize their work with time."

Light lined up the times neatly and went back to the Fire of Wisdom. The first moment of the first second of the first minute of the first hour of the first day of time, he took the head of the Fire of Wisdom in his hands and made a luminous and tall warrior from it. The eyes of the angels sparkled with excitement and joy; finally, a warrior who was unparalleled in purity and transparency stood before them.

Don't think it was as easy as I am recounting for you today. No! The creation and completion of this beautiful warrior took from the very first moment of time, which coincided with the beginning of spring, until the middle of this season. But well, when the work was done, the hard helmet and armor that were on the warrior's body amazed all the angels.

The demons of Darkness, who were still standing on the edge of the dark world, looked at the beauty of the warrior with regret and sighed. Of course, this sigh made Darkness curious, and brought him from the very bottom to the edge of the dark world, where he stood next to the other demons to watch.

Suddenly, Light took a breath and with a deep exhale, breathed consciousness and spirit into the sky.[23] The Sky-Warrior opened his eyes in the breath and his blue gaze flowed all over the world.[24]

Light said to the angels: "Look at him well. The name of this warrior is Sky."[25] And he turned to Sky: "Do you know why I brought you into existence? To watch over everyone from above the world. Especially watch the behavior of the demons who are watching us from below."

Sky lowered his head and saw the demons and Darkness down there and of course, since his existence was made of the Fire of Wisdom, he smiled with joy as soon as he made eye contact with Darkness. So, Darkness became agitated with seeing that one smile.

*

Curious angels were circling around Sky and were inspecting him well. Light again put his hand among the flames of the Fire of Wisdom and brought out the flames in the form of small fiery balls. He scattered them on the helmet and armor of Sky.

Now the body of Sky was covered with luminous balls and the angels were more excited than before, staring at Sky.

Light said: "These fiery balls are called Stars. See that luminous ball that I have placed higher than all the stars. That is the Moon. Look at that shining and big ball that is on the helmet—the one whose light has illuminated the entire sky. I have named it the sun."

And with the last sentence, Light blew into the sun and the sun warmed up. Light blew into the moon and it took light. He blew into the stars and they took a fresh breath like new soldiers.

For the Sky-Warrior and his soldiers to come to life, it was time to create water.[26] This time, Light took the tear of the eye of the Fire of Wisdom between his fingers and spread it in the blue gaze of the sky and expanded it. Finally, in the early summer the water, which was unparalleled in transparency and clarity, flowed under the sky and reflected the purity and beauty of the sky and the stars on itself like a mirror with the breath of Light.

Now it was time for the tranquility of the earth to appear between the sky and the water. In this way, Light took a flame from the feet of the Fire of Wisdom and smoothed it well to resemble a piece of land. Then he put that piece of land on the water and caressed it with his fingers to grow from all sides.

It was the beginning of autumn when Light blew on the earth. With that breath, the heart of the earth softened to accept the first seed and give life to the first plant with the power of its existence!

At the same time, Light called the Sky-Warrior to take a thin beam of light from the small stars on his chest and make a delicate plant with it—a magical plant that had the seed of all plants in it and was created to be the mother of all plants in the world.

Light put the luminous plant on the ground and firmly rooted it in the dry land among the water. He brought his head close to the plant and said: "I name you All-Seed. You have the seed of all plants in your heart. One day all the trees and fresh flowers will grow from your existence and the world will be drowned in happiness and beauty."

Light took a deep breath and blew on the stem of the plant. The plant took life in the breath. The mother of the plants raised her stem and opened her leaves under the sunlight. All-Seed was so delicately made that she didn't have even a bit of husk and chaff on her stem. The luminous stars looked at the delicacy of the plant, and their hearts warmed with love!

Light's work to create the world was not over yet. Now he took a flame from the right hand of the Fire of Wisdom and worked to make a small cube from the middle of autumn to the beginning of winter.

The small cube was as luminous as the moon and with the breath of Light, opened its eyes to the world. Light caressed the cube with abundant love and said: "You are a cow! A good cow that is supposed to be the father of all animals on earth and of course the father of all creatures that fly in the sky and swim in the water!"

The white cow[27] looked at itself and stared at the moonlight in the sky for a while. It repeated Light's words several times and seemed to suddenly understand that the rest of the animals, meaning horses, giraffes, cats, fish, even eagles, and everything and everything, are supposed to come from it. Then it sighed and laughed with joy![28]

● ● ●

Light gently stroked the cow's back and continued: "Good cow! I want to send you to earth with a creature named Human. I want you to always be with him and not leave him alone. If you do not leave the human alone, both of you will always live happily."

The cow repeated Light's words again and understood that it had to wait for a companion named Human, and then it nodded confidently.

*

The angels circled around Light to see what amazing creature Light wanted to create this time—a creature that was named Human.

Light waited a bit and thought to create a creature that would help expand endless joy and be the source of knowledge and wisdom. In this way, how much better and more beautiful the world would be!

So, Light again reached out to the Fire of Wisdom and took a flame from the left hand of the Fire. He nurtured the flame with his fingers so that it became soft and fluid. After that he added some awareness like a white light to the middle of the flame and nurtured the flame so much again that the color of the flame also became as white as awareness.

He continued this work until the end of winter and at the beginning of spring, the human was ready. Light only had to breathe in him to wake him up to see the world!

You won't believe it, but the human was as beautiful and radiant as the sun. Light named the human Keyumars.[29]

"Keyumars, I want you to be the father of humans on earth.[30] I want you to promise to take care of the cow. In a not-so-distant time, you will need it to prepare food and clothing, and to live."

Keyumars listened carefully to Light's words. He sharpened his ears and narrowed his eyes and tried to focus on every word he heard. In the end, he didn't know the meaning of many of the words he heard! For example, he didn't know what food or clothing was. Keyumars had just woken up and had no experience of hunger, cold, heat, or any other event in the world. However, because Light had given him knowledge, he could almost feel every word.

*

The creation of the world ended.

Darkness was sitting at the very bottom of the edge of the dark world. He admired the joy and light spread by the angels in the sky and the earth. But happiness and laughter also added to his greed and anger.

With every look at Light's creations, Darkness harbored resentment and plotted their destruction. Darkness now realized that its demons were too big and bulky to step into Light's delicate world. So, he had to create demons and fairies with smaller bodies so they could infiltrate the sky and earth and pave the way for major impurities.

Darkness returned to the depths of the dark world and created tiny and filthy creatures from tangled darkness. Thousands and thousands of beetles, thousands and thousands of snakes, thousands and thousands of spiders, thousands and thousands of scorpions, thousands and thousands of flies, thousands and thousands of lizards, thousands and thousands of worms, thousands and thousands of locusts, and thousands and thousands of insects and other stingers.

When the work was done, he said to the demons: "Look what a complete army I have! With your help, I will never allow Darkness to disappear. I will show Light with these small annoying soldiers how all its joys will be destroyed. I promise all of you that with the destruction of Light, we will take over all of its world!"

Then Darkness commanded those thousands and thousands of stinging and crawling creatures to attack the sky, water, and earth and darken the world with their presence.

*

In the blink of an eye, those tiny filthy creatures entered the Light-world through every hole.

Insects flew all over the sky and stole the blue gaze of the sky. The earth was also full of harmful stingers that did not allow the pleasant light to shine on the earth and water. The earth and sky completely lost their light and color!

Seeing all this ugliness, Light created the angel Wind from the Fire of Wisdom and prepared an army of warrior angels to ride on the back of the wind and go out to defend the sky, water, and earth.

*

Wind blew and carried the angels everywhere in the world. It spun so much in the sky that the insects were scattered. The warrior angels also divided into several groups and with each other's help, they brought drops of water to the sky and towards the sun.

The sun shone brighter than ever and the drops of water evaporated and made cotton-like clouds.

With the formation of clouds and the rain pouring from their hearts, Light commanded the angel of Wind to move the clouds.

Wind blew again and with its long hands took the corners of the clouds and pulled them in the sky. Now raindrops were raining everywhere in the sky and earth and washing the world.

The sky shone and the clean earth was found again. Although the angels could not eliminate all the insects, they were pleased to have helped. After the rain, a large number of those insects and reptiles had burrowed into the earth and made themselves secured inside the earth. Some of them also flew and were safe from rain and wind. That's why, despite the heavy rains, we can still see all kinds of insects and stingers in our world today. Although we shouldn't worry too much. They are not so many that they take over all the sky and earth or compete with the joy of the world.

*

Darkness—which had seen defeat—came out of his hole with great anger to enter the happy world of Light from the hole created in the sky. This was one of those things that no one believed!

The angels saw him standing in the middle of their world and overthrowing the beauties. Who would believe that Darkness could stand in the middle of the world of Light?

Darkness was staring in an unbelievable silence. He seemed to stand there for a few days. But suddenly he came to himself and ran in front of the astonished eyes of the angels. He hit the earth hard with great speed—so hard that the earth shook and a crack was created in it!

Do you know what he was thinking about these few days? By creating a crack in the earth, he could ruin it and put the earth out of work.

He hit again and again, hard and harder into that crack, and pushed the earth hard. He was unaware that with the cracking and wrinkling of the earth on this side of the earth, a beautiful mountain range had grown and risen on the other side of the earth.

Light and the angels, who from the very top of the sky saw the struggle of Darkness to destroy the earth, laughed a lot. Because Darkness, without knowing or wanting to, had given the earth a better and more beautiful shape!

With the growth of mountains around the earth, running waters and rivers could easily reach each other and irrigate all the earth. It was enough for angel Khordad to keep the path of the rivers clean. So, the world had become more beautiful and better.

Even Darkness did not know that the roots of the mountains were knotted to each other under the earth and did not know that his blows had made the earth stronger than before—something that made angel Spandarmaz happy.

*

The sound of celebration—with the growth of mountains and the flow of rivers—went up. Darkness—which had become angrier than before and was ashamed of his ignorance for making mountains—roared and returned to the dark world.

*

Light blew into the new mountains and rivers and named the new mountains Alborz[31]. He allowed the mountains to grow up to the sky for eight hundred years. Thus, Alborz grew.

Darkness, who could not take his eyes off the mountains, became so mad that he created a few more demons to perhaps be able to destroy the plant, cow, and human as soon as possible in retaliation for all this goodness in the world!

Darkness created a demon to put the Light-world to sleep during the day. Then he brought the demon of disease into existence, and after that, the demon of death[32]. The demons were created one after another to obey the command of Darkness. With all these new demons, Darkness had no doubt that he would win!

He sent the demons of disease and death towards the All-Seed plant. The demons circled around the plant and the plant slowly dried up and her lifeless body fell to the ground.

The angels were worried and looked at Light to help All-Seed. But Light was completely calm, as if a good thing like the growth of mountains was on the way.

After that, the sun shone on the plant and a day passed until the body of the plant cracked and the seeds of all kinds of plants, trees, and flowers were freed from the delicate stem of the All-Seed plant.

Then Wind spun and blew on the seeds by the command of Light. He scattered all the seeds over the earth. Finally, the sun shone, the water flowed, and angel Amordad stood guard so that new plants would grow all over the earth from the seeds.

Darkness was staring at the upper world with wide eyes. Now the world was covered with the greenery of trees and the joy of colorful flowers. And all of this had only one reason: the invasion of Darkness into the world of Light!

Darkness had been defeated again but was still hopeful that could bring down the cow and destroy the joy of the cow and human at the same time.

He sent the demon of death after the cow.

The demon of death quietly approached the cow and entered the cow's body like a deep breath. The cow's body became as hard as stone and could no longer move. Its legs were stuck to the ground and its tongue was not moving in its mouth. It couldn't even wag its tail. Due to extreme weakness, it fell to the ground and died.

Light asked Bahman to take the soul of the cow[33] to the sky so that the moonlight would shine on it. Angel Bahman, who was in charge of taking care of the animals, went to the soul of the cow and was careful not to let the demons reach it.

The soul of the cow was taken to the moon and the moonlight made it shine. But the cow's body dried up under the sunshine.

The earth opened its mouth and the dried body of the cow sank into the soil. Then the sun shone on the soil, and the rain fell, and medicinal plants[34] grew from the cow's body—plants that helped people to stay away from the harm of the demon of disease.

Now, according to the law of the world of Light, even the lifeless body of the cow was helping humans by giving them medicinal plants. The time had come for other animals to come from the good cow and spread throughout the earth, sky, and water.

Darkness cursed the earth, sky, water, and all the animals that had come from the cow. He commanded the demon of death to kill Keyumars. He thought that with the death of Keyumars, there would be no human left to work on creating endless joy and wisdom.

He thought that with the destruction of the Human, the existence of this world would be futile for Light!

*

The demon of death quietly crawled on the ground, approached Keyumars, and slowly entered his body from the little toe of his right foot.

Keyumars' body trembled with the entrance of the demon. He had lost the ability to move his legs and could not take a step.

Death went up from Keyumars' legs and entered his stomach. Suddenly Keyumars felt a severe hunger and thirst but could not move his body to eat or drink anything. His body was completely dry and motionless.

In a short time, the demon took control of the entire human and entered his head.

With the entrance of the demon into his head, Keyumars' eyes went black. He had never experienced such a state until then, so he could only close his eyes.

Keyumars fell to the ground and died.

Darkness had killed Keyumars and none of Light's soldiers had been able to prevent the death of the human. Darkness was waiting to celebrate Light's defeat with the moaning and wailing of the angels.

But no matter how long Darkness waited, there was no news of sadness or mourning!

Instead, the sky was bluer than ever, and the angels were circling around the stars. The rivers were flowing, the colorful flowers were perfuming everything, and of course, the sun was shining brighter than ever on Keyumars' body and drying his body and. . .

Light? Light acted as if there was no dead man. His mind was completely at ease!

Darkness stared at the world above, and forty years passed.

*

During these forty years, a rhubarb plant grew from the side of Keyumars. Darkness looked at Keyumars' body and the growth of the rhubarb stem with astonishment and focus for forty years.

Darkness was worried that like the All-Seed plant or the cow, Keyumars could also bring more humans into existence, humans who would spread all over the earth and fill the world with joy. And these thoughts brought him anxiety and nausea.

Finally, the stem of the rhubarb reached the sky. Another fifty years passed in the same state, and Darkness was still staring at the rhubarb with concern.

The sun shone and gave its warmth to the earth until the stem of the rhubarb was divided into two parts. Each part was like the body of a human firmly embracing another body.

Days passed, and with the passage of time, the faces of humans appeared on the two bodies. This was when Darkness realized that the human race still existed. So, anger drove him mad again.

As much as Darkness was madly angry, Light was happy.

● ● ●

Light blew calmly and steadily on the bodies of the rhubarb plant, which now looked exactly like humans, and called them "Mashya" and "Mashyaneh"[35] in their ears.

Mashya and Mashyaneh slowly opened their eyes under the sunlight and saw angels around them, welcoming them.

Light introduced them as the father and mother of the human race.

Darkness took a grudge against the continuation of the human race. He vowed to turn the world into a dark place for the human race.[36]

*

Mashya and Mashyaneh accompanied the angels[37], but Keyumars' body was still lying on the earth.

The sun shone day by day by the command of Light and melted Keyumars' body. And the earth accepted the melted body.

When the entire body of Keyumars sank into the earth, each part of it turned into one of the metals: gold, silver, iron, copper, zinc, and many others.[38]

Suddenly the earth shook and the metals spread under the soils all over the world so that humans and their children could one day make agricultural tools with them and live more happily than before.

*

With the help of the envy and anger of Darkness, the whole world was drowned in complete beauty. Now plants, animals, and humans were striving to acquire the knowledge of life, and joy was flowing more than ever on earth.

Despite this, Darkness sat at the very bottom of the world, in the darkness of ignorance and unawareness. He looked up at the top of the world with anger, regret, and sometimes astonishment, and drew thousands of destruction plans.

2. The Angel of Wind

Light created the Angel of Wind[39] so beautifully that all creatures of the world admired him. The young Wind was the most vibrant angel of heaven and earth. He wore a green dress and light wooden shoes. His presence was so pleasant and his face so beautiful that he brought comfort and goodness to all creatures in heaven and earth.

When Light sent Wind to the earth, he whispered to Wind that his power lay in his agility and gentleness. Wind is so agile that he can move faster than other creatures and so gentle that sometimes no one notices his presence.

That's why people usually don't feel the entrance of the Angel of Wind into their bodies. Perhaps they have become accustomed to inviting the freshness and vitality of the Wind into themselves with their breaths, but they do not notice his presence.

• • •

The delicate Wind flows in the body of creatures at every moment and with every breath, and is aware of everyone's heart.

Light told Wind that when he passes through a warm place like a desert, he should become warm. When he passes through snow and mountains, he should become as cold as snow. When he passes through a fragrant place, he should take the pleasant smell of that place with him. This way, in motion and movement, Wind could become one with every part of the world of Light and be pleasant and delightful at the moment.

The Wind was admirable!

＊

Days passed one after another. The Angel of Wind roamed the whole world and everything became as it should be. So, he became a symbol of adaptability in the beautiful world of Light.

He did his job so well that if he passed through the sea, he took the freshness of the waves and the smell of the water. He wandered on the beach, bringing peace. He twisted in the mountains, amplifying the hardness and stability of the mountain, and wherever he wandered among the trees in the forest, he spread the scent of the leaves. And when smelling flowers, the scent of the flowers permeated him.

He always caressed humans, animals, plants, earth, and sky, and gave comfort to all of them. He set the clouds in motion in the sky and spread the rain on the earth.

In a word, Wind made the world fresher than before and Darkness could not stand the presence of the good Wind. He created a demon to confront the Wind and named it the Black-Wind.

The soul of the Black-Wind was from the soul of Darkness. The Black-Wind was empty of thought, and full of bustling. Darkness had shaped the Black-Wind in the complexity of anger and enmity. As a result, it was an agile but heavy creature—a prisoner in a strange contradiction.

The heavy hard Black-Wind demon came to the world to be present everywhere like the Angel of Wind. Contrary to the Angel of Wind, it destroyed everything that brought comfort to the world and its inhabitants.

The Black-Wind twisted quickly into a storm and rebelled against the whole world. Wherever it saw beauty, it threw the heaviness of its breath on it.

It was able to destroy many lives, ruin houses, and flatten crops.

It spun madly, and wherever it passed dust rose, trees were uprooted, large black clouds were made in the sky, and it caused a strange calamity.

It wasn't long before people knew that the Black-Wind was an invisible and filthy demon and had no intention other than destruction.

But people did not know a way to fight that stormy and wild demon.

All animals, plants, humans, and even angels were bewildered by the Black-Wind and its strange features. Only Darkness was enjoying his new soldier.

*

When Darkness saw that he could scare everyone with the help of the Black-Wind, he ordered it to enter the body of humans and animals like a hard and cold breath.

Darkness wanted the Black-Wind to take comfort from people. In this way, the demon of death could also do its job more easily.

Light, which was wise, became aware of the dirty thoughts of Darkness and did not sit idly. Light gave the Angel of Wind more power to be able to stand against the Black-Wind.

So, the two winds twisted into each other wherever and whenever they met each other, and a hard battle began.

It wasn't long before the Black-Wind fell in front of the infinite power of the Wind Angel. He returned to the dark world and confessed that he had no power left and had to stop destroying!

Light—was relieved— ordered the angels to give the magical power of courage to the whole world as a gift so that the people could face the demon of death and not be afraid of it.

Then, the power of hope and the world after death were created above the world of Light. And people learned that despite the demon of death, the light of wisdom and joy does not end, and life remains above the world of Light.

*

When creatures felt able to confront the demon of death, Light also bestowed two other valuable gifts to people: tolerance and forgetfulness.

With these valuable gifts, people could endure pain. And most likely, after a while they would forget, so that the sorrow of suffering would not continue over time.

In this way, generation after generation, humans learned that eventually, comfort and joys will take the place of all pains. So, they fought hopefully with the army of Darkness to find more joy.

3. Rain and Angel Tishtrya [40]

Darkness executes his plans one after another to plunge the world into destruction. He is angry and has prepared an army of black demons, fairies, and witches[41], ready to wage war against Light at any moment.

One of these wars, which occurs annually between the armies of Light and Darkness, is the battle over rainfall.

*

When Light created the Sky Warrior and created the stars from the flames of the Fire of Wisdom, he sewed the stars like military medals on Sky's attire.

Later, Light gave life to the luminous stars and they became the angels. These angels were like soldiers under the command of the Sky Warrior, and like a united army, were always ready to fight to save the world from the onslaught of the Darkness-army.

One of those beautiful stars, which was seen shining large from the earth, was a brave soldier named the Angel Tishtrya.

Angel Tishtrya was a tall, young warrior on the chest of the sky. Light entrusted him with an important task: to oversee the rainfall.

Raindrops were pure, and that unparalleled purity had the power to eliminate the creeping and biting creatures of the Darkness-army.

Rainfall was also important for plant growth and agricultural blessings. We know when plants grow with abundant water and sufficient rain, agriculture thrives, and the food of humans and animals is easily harvested from the earth. Thus, people's lives continue. As a result, awareness and joy grow in the world.

Darkness realized that rain is important for the stability of the world of Light. So, he plotted to create drought and famine.

*

The angels were arranging everything for the first rainfall. The sun shone more, and the heat increased. The sea water evaporated, went to the sky, and the angels arranged the clouds next to each other to let the first raindrops fall from the heart of the sky.

In those days, each raindrop was as large as a tall human to better irrigate the earth. As the years passed the size of the raindrops became smaller until they reached their current size. Anyway, it was raining, and Angel Tishtrya was watching from above the sky to ensure the purity of the rain, and the growing of the plants.

But Tishtrya and the soldier angels were not the only ones watching the rain! Darkness had his eyes on the sky from his world and realized with the first rainfall that he had to stop this event.

Darkness sent a demon named Apush[42] to stand against the clouds. The demon Apush was big and powerful—so big that if he stood in the sky and put his hands under the clouds, no drop would reach the earth! And of course, he did just that. He opened his hands. The raindrops fell into the palms of the demon, gathering there, and no more drops reached the earth.

Angel Tishtrya looked at the height and width of the demon and saw that he could not free the drops from Apush's hands alone. So, he called the Angel of Wind.

Wind went to the sky and, with his long hands, took the corners of the clouds and moved them. Then he filled his lips with air and blew into the palms of the demon to free the raindrops.

Suddenly, the demon Apush saw that his hands were empty and the clouds were going from above his head to another corner of the sky!

By this time, Apush saw that Angel Tishtrya and the Wind were ready to fight him.

The demon Apush thought, "Why have they become two?" He lowered his head and called a demon from the dark world to his aid. Apush would go to war with the warrior Tishtrya.

That big demon that Apush called was named Spangarosh[43], who opened his hands under the clouds to block the path of the rain. Spangarosh asked other small demons to help them. Angel Tishtrya looked at the number of demons and had no choice except to ask Fire[44] to fight the small demons.

Fire, with mace in hand, hid among the whiteness of the clouds to ambush the demons.

A tumultuous war began!

On one side, the demons were approaching the clouds one after another to take the clouds from the Angel of Wind and stop the rain. On the other hand, Wind was moving the clouds with great power, and Fire was also striking the mace hard on the demons' heads.

Since the mace of Fire was of its own kind, with each strike, a flame would jump in the sky. And with each flame, one wounded demon would let out a loud cry.

Of course, today we call that cry and flame thunder and lightning. It seems that this war in the sky is still ongoing!

*

From the start of this battle, ten nights passed. Tishtrya transformed himself from the stature of a warrior soldier into a bull with golden horns to show his increased power to the enemy.

With this physical transformation, the power to rain also increased. Therefore, the rain washed away a large number of dark crawlers and biters who were walking on the earth or flying in the sky. Many drowned in the rainwater. But some of them also went into holes in the earth and survived.

● ● ●

From the carcasses of those insects and crawlers that perished, a poison flowed on the earth and desert soil came into existence—soil that did not accept any plant.

Also, some of that poison, along with the rainwater, joined the flow of rivers and seas. It made the taste of the seas salty.

Eventually, so much rain fell that it washed the dark poison from the sky, and a large sea called the Frakhkart[45] came into existence, which at that time exactly covered one-third of the earth.[46]

After twenty nights of fighting, Tishtrya needed more speed and agility and appeared as a white horse with golden hooves. He ran across the sky and earth to make sure that everywhere was clean from pollution.

Tishtrya told the soldier angels, "Now is the time for agricultural rain. The fields and gardens are waiting. Try to keep the demons away from the clouds!"

He plunged his golden hooves into the Frakhkart and galloped through the water. From the hustle and bustle of Tishtrya and the turbulence of the water, a white foam formed on the sea.

Tishtrya took that foam to the sky to make a big cloud—a cloud to irrigate the agricultural lands so that more plants would grow. More fruitful plants were needed than before, to compensate for the lost plants in the poisoned desert soils.

Apush was ready for war! He turned himself into a black horse and also entered the Frakhkart. Two horses—a soldier angel and a big demon—faced each other. One was neighing and the other was striking the water with its hooves.

The two horses charged at each other and hit each other's bodies with heavy blows for three nights. Tishtrya, who had a smaller stature, lost the power to fight after three days, and on the third day was thrown out of the sea by a blow from the demon Apush.

The wounded white horse went to the top of the sky with sorrow to meet Light. Light, who was aware of everything, bestowed more amazing power on Tishtrya, a power that distinguished this angel from other soldier stars. Tishtrya had to save the earth from drought.

Light assured Tishtrya that the power of thousands of horses was flowing in his muscles and throughout his body. Light promised him, as long

● ● ●

as the world of Light is stable, this amazing power will make him the victor of the battlefield.

In the blink of an eye, Tishtrya's body shone, and his muscles became stronger and more prominent. There was no trace of wounds on his body.

The angel returned to the Frakhkart and stood face to face with the demon Apush. This time, the white horse struck the black horse so hard that he threw him out of the sea. Now the demon Apush, wounded, had fallen to the ground, and seeing the magical power of Tishtrya, he had to accept defeat.

Powerful Tishtrya was alone in the sea, and there was little time to gather the white foam from the sea. This was because the fields were thirsty, and the earth needed more plants to provide food for all creatures.

*

Light—witnessing Angel Tishtrya's effort—sent the Three-legged Donkey to assist him. The Three-legged Donkey set foot on the earth with amazing powers. He could stir the water by waving his hooves or let out a deafening cry to agitate the sea. Then the hidden Darkness in the sea would surface and be destroyed.

Three-legged Donkey had a white body, the height of a mountain, and large humps on his back. He had two ears and one horn on his head, and not an ordinary horn, but a horn that had a thousand other horns growing on it! With two eyes on his face, two eyes above his head, and two eyes on either side of his humps, he was seeing the world and thus watched over everything and everyone.

On his body, nine mouths could be seen. Three mouths on his head, three mouths on his humps, three mouths on his sides, for eating and talking.

It's really hard to imagine: I know!

The Three-legged Donkey lived in the Frakhkart from that day on. If the dark demons fancied polluting the sea, they would have to fight with him.

*

In this way, an important collaboration took shape in the Light-world. Tishtrya and the Three-legged Donkey stirred the water, and white foam floated on the sea waves. Tishtrya gathered the foam with a scoop the size of his sky hat and took it to the sky. The soldier angels turned the foam into clouds.

Very soon, with such an organized effort, the rainfall started again.

The demons returned to the Darkness-world, tired and hopeless. Nevertheless, Darkness was still hopeful that could defeat the army of Light.

Oh! Darkness's plans were not over. He had decided to neutralize the sun's heat. This is how the Cold-Demon came into existence.

*

The Cold-Demon stepped into the place of the clouds in the sky. He was a little different from the other demons. Cold didn't need to attack anything or use any special power to fight the angels. He could just be standing there and the cold was everywhere!

The Cold-Demon stood next to the clouds, and in an instant, such cold was created that the raindrops froze and turned into snow and hail. Having finished his mission in the sky, he went straight to the earth and sat on the ground.

In an instant, the earth and plants fell asleep from the cold.

The Fire on the cloud[47] had just realized: This demon is not wild like the other demons and is actually lazy, heavy, and bored. Then the Fire swung his mace in the air and hit the clouds to wake them up from sleep with this blow.

The mace's blow was so effective and burning that the clouds jumped out of sleep all at once. However, Light—which was wiser than all—had a new idea. He told the soldier angels, the clouds, and Fire and Wind: "This time when the clouds fall asleep, do nothing. Let the rain freeze and turn into snow. Then get to work. The Angel of Wind must take the clouds to the mountains. The Fire on the cloud must also remain calm so that more snow falls on the mountains."

The angels understood that Light knew the Light-world better than anyone else. So, they just watched. Light had his usual smile on his lips and said: "You will see how much the lazy Cold-Demon helps us to reduce the trouble of the soldier angels and Tishtrya."

*

Snow covered the mountains, and it was what Light had predicted:

The Cold-Demon returned to the sky. The Angel of Wind took the clouds to the mountains. The snows whitened the mountains, and when the sun came back in the sky, the snows calmly turned into water and joined the rivers, the rivers that brought water to more fields and plants.

*

Darkness looked up again; now the soldiers of Light had put his Cold-Demon to work. They were storing enough water for agriculture by accumulating snow on the mountain peaks.

In this way, the plan of Darkness again benefited the freshness of the world and the joy of the people.

4. Sleeping in the World of Light

Light, from above the world, was observing the work and efforts of humans and animals. He realized that with each passing day, the speed of work and the physical abilities of creatures were diminishing. It seemed as if they had become bored and lacked their previous vitality. Their laughter no longer reached the ears of Light and the angels.

Humans were sitting and the quadrupeds didn't even have the ability to chew food. No more sheep were giving milk, and the oxen were not pulling. Birds were not flying at all and were not singing.

Light named this condition fatigue and had to look for a way to bring joy back to their lives.

For this reason, he created Sleep, to bring vitality back to the world.

*

The face of Sleep seemed to be about fifteen years old. His eyes were completely white and his body was transparent and almost invisible. If you looked at one side of his body, you could almost see the other side!

While Light was naming Sleep, he blew on his face. Sleep opened his white eyes and looked curiously at the new world he had stepped into.

The angels lined up in front of Sleep and were staring at him.

After all this time and all these events, when Light created something to help the angels or humans, everyone watched in amazement.

You know, they were getting more and more surprised each time!

In short, they examined Sleep from head to toe, and they all came to the conclusion that Sleep is a wonderful, vibrant, and pleasant creature, just like the feeling people experience after sleeping.

Light said to Sleep: "I want to send you to humans and animals to make them as powerful and strong as before. I send you to bring life back to the earth. Good Sleep, no one on earth will ever see you! So, when humans and animals are tired, go to their side with peace of mind. They will feel your gentleness and it will become difficult for them to stay awake. Wait for their eyes to close completely and their breaths to get longer. Then go into their eyes and ears so they can dream and get the most pleasure from sleeping."

And Light created a new joy for the world called a dream, because sleeping was one of the ways to create joy for creatures.

Sleep became curious after hearing this word and asked, "Only humans and animals? But aren't the rest of the army of Light also striving? Why shouldn't I go to the plants so they can rest?"

Angel Amordad came forward and explained to Sleep, "Plants don't get tired. Their life is much shorter than their sleep. Good Sleep! When the Cold demon comes and brings winter, the plants die. They come back to life in the spring with the warmth of the sun. They don't need sleep in this short life. Plants, although they seem more delicate than humans and animals, are happier and fresher than them. Do you know why? Because they experience more generosity. They make sure no one in the world goes hungry and this generosity creates joy for them."

Sleep asked again, "So what about the earth? The earth that has to bear the weight of the whole world all day and night? She, who holds all these mountains, rivers, humans, animals, and plants, must get tired!"

Angel Spandarmaz—the kind angel of the earth—smiled. "You shouldn't put the earth to sleep. If the earth goes to sleep, all living creatures will perish. Time is lost. Plants do not grow. If the plant is not green, then all humans, quadrupeds, and many other animals do not have food to eat. We all know everyone will perish. The earth is always awake and gets her life force from love and generosity!"

Sleep thought: "Rain, rivers, seas, waters! Don't they need sleep?"

Angel Anahita[48] and Angel Khordad came forward. Anahita gently said, "Pleasant Sleep! If you go to the running waters and put them to sleep, there will be no flow of life left in the world. The sea that sleeps becomes a swamp. The river that sleeps dies!"

Angel Khordad continued, "If they are not there, the fields and plants will perish. Humans and animals also become thirsty and lifeless. Waters must always be awake and flowing. They get their life force from their purity!"

This time Sleep asked with hesitation, "Everything you said is true, but Wind and Fire must need sleep! If they are not in the world for a while, nothing will change. Right?"

Angel Wind spun around and put his hand on Sleep's shoulder. "The Wind must always be awake. The Wind is the caress of Light on the world. If the Wind sleeps, the devils can easily destroy the sky, clouds, and rain. Don't forget, the breath of living creatures is the flow of the Wind. If the Wind sleeps, everyone dies. Breath gets its life force from hope!"

Angel Ardibehesht and Angel Atur[49], who were the guardians of Fire, kindly took Sleep's hand in theirs. "If Fire sleeps, a world falls apart and the Light dies. The stars, moon, and sun go out. Knowledge and wisdom are lost and a world without them will never have endless joy. Without Fire, the power of Darkness to destroy the world increases. Fire is alive with knowledge, purity, love, forgiveness, sacrifice, and hope for the salvation of endless joy!"

Finally, Sleep understood that he should not put any of the Light-army to sleep except for humans and animals.

*

In this way, Sleep traveled to all cities, villages, and hamlets. He visited every corner of the world and gathered his senses so that no one would feel his presence.

He would quietly sit above humans and animals and caress them to feel calm and close their eyes. After days of wakefulness and work, the taste of comfort and pleasure of Sleep was very sweet for everyone.

But unfortunately, Sleep was so sweet that people wanted to spend their entire lives sleeping.

Ardibehesht—who was in charge of controlling and organizing the world—noticed the laziness and idleness of some people. So, he came to earth to establish a new law for wakefulness and sleep in the world with the help of Shahrivar.

The new law stated that humans are only allowed to sleep at night and must wake up early every day and enjoy work under the sunlight!

• • •

In this way, balance and order returned to the world for a while. But Darkness thought of a new idea. He thought of another temptation to destroy the beauty of struggle and effort.

He sent the tired demon "Boushasp"[50] to earth.

*

Boushasp was a strange demon. He would sit quietly at night, waiting for the morning and exactly when dreams and Sleep left people alone, he would go to their side.

He would whisper in people's ears the temptation of seeing new dreams or make their eyelids so heavy that they did not want to see the morning sunlight!

Some people were listening to Boushasp's temptation, and slept for a few minutes with his black magic. But unfortunately, when they opened their eyes, they saw that the day had passed and they were very lazy and idle—as if they hadn't slept at all.

The reason for this fatigue and exhaustion is clear. They were experiencing sleep with the temptation of the lazy Boushasp[51].

Ardibehesht took another look at the earth and saw that the order of the world had been disrupted by Boushasp. The lazy people were so immersed in sleep that they had been left behind from effort and learning, so much so that even the soldier angels could not stand against the sleepy people. For this reason, the complaint of people's laziness reached Light.

Light said to Ardibehesht, Shahrivar, and all the soldier angels, "You have to give humans the opportunity to learn honesty, order, and effort themselves. They have to choose their own way of life and stand against the demons and their temptations. This is not your battle with Darkness. It is the battle of the conscious Human and Darkness. Let humans choose vigilance and effort themselves!"

But the angels asked Light for help again. The insistence of the angels caused Light not to turn them down and although he knew that human wisdom was enough to fight with Boushasp, he created an animal called the rooster and sent it to earth.

The rooster would sing the wake-up call every morning with the sunrise and sing for the vigilance of people against the demon's temptations.

In addition, a soldier angel named Oushbam[52] came to earth from the sun.

*

You may not know, but for years, Oushbam has been standing next to people after the end of their nightly dreams. While Boushasp whispers the temptation of laziness, Oushbam sings a song of vitality and vigilance.

*

It seems you have understood that after the death of Keyumars, the war between Darkness and Humans is fought over awareness and nothing else!

Now it is up to humans to choose whether to shake hands with Boushasp or angel Oushbam.

5. The Children of Keyumars:

Siyamak[53] and Hushang[54]

As you read in the first story: Darkness sent the demon of death to Keyumars, the first human.

Death entered Keyumars' body from the little toe of the right foot. Suddenly, his foot dried up and he was left unable to walk. Then, death entered his stomach and for the first time in his life, Keyumars experienced hunger and thirst[55].

Death ascended in Keyumars' body to the point where it took control of his chest, shoulders, and head, preventing the first human from moving his body parts.

Keyumars lay motionless and lifeless on the ground for a while. The sound of Darkness laughing at this small victory echoed in the dark world. Light watched everything, smiling at Darkness's ignorance and helplessness.

Keyumars' lifeless body sparkled in the sunlight. The sun shone for forty years until a plant called the rhubarb grew from Keyumars' body and reached towards the sky.

The strange rhubarb's stems were the bodies of two intertwined humans. One stem was named "Mashya" and the other "Mashyaneh".

Another fifty years passed until the two stems developed into complete humans and began their life on earth, becoming the parents of the human race.

Mashya and Mashyaneh brought a child into the world whom they named Siyamak, ninety-three years and six months from the time they became human.

Siyamak was a soldier of the army of Light. He was aware that Darkness would take advantage of every opportunity to invade the world. For this reason, he asked Light and the angels to give him the power to triumph over the foul demons.

The angels bestowed upon Siyamak an amazing power, and Siyamak gained the strength of a hundred strong men.[56] He fought with the demons for days and years and emerged victorious.

However, one day, he fell into a lethargic sleep. He became oblivious to his surroundings, and the shadow of the demon of death fell upon his face. Then the bad Black-Wind demon entered Siyamak's breaths, and eventually, the demon of death managed to overcome his life.

*

Before his death, Siyamak had taught his son Hushang everything about the world of Light, the angels, the earth, the sky and water, plants, and animals.

Hushang, like his father, desired to be a warrior and fight the demons. He wanted to avenge Siyamak's death from Darkness. So, he went to the heights of the world, that is, to Mount Alborz, and from there, he called out to Light and the angel of the waters.

*

After some time, the angel of the waters, who was a kind lady, passed through the sky with her chariot carried by four strong horses. Seeing Hushang, she descended from Mount Alborz.

The angel of the waters was named Anahita[57]. She was a beautiful lady with a long white dress, golden shoes, earrings made of gold, and a crown with a hundred shining jewels.[58]

Anahita descended from her chariot to listen to Hushang's words. Hushang had heard about Anahita's kindness and generosity from his father and was seeing her up close for the first time. He incredulously looked at her swift horses, which were made of rain, hail, cloud, and wind.[59]

Anahita, who had previously assisted Siyamak in the battle against the demons and was aware of Hushang's request, stood waiting for the young man's words.

Hushang took his eyes off the horses and suddenly found himself looking into the eyes of Anahita. He was in front of a representative of the Light and should not miss the opportunity to talk. The young man, excitement evident in his voice, asked the pure lady of the waters for more power than other humans so that he could, like his father, overcome the demons, fairies, and everything that came from the dark world. He sincerely wanted to have a magical power to protect other humans.

*

Anahita praised Hushang's bravery and eagerness to help other humans. She was aware that angel Bahman would guard his thoughts and angel Spandarmaz would fully understand the value of his sacrifices.

So, she reminded Hushang that he would receive the gift of magical power only if he could place truth and righteousness as the law of his life. Then he could also triumph over the dark army!

Hushang believed in these words, and at that moment he sent a light of wisdom[60] towards Mount Alborz. The light of wisdom was placed in the hands of Anahita.

Pure wisdom was so radiant that the young man could not take his eyes off it for a moment. Anahita placed the light above Hushang's head and reminded him that as long as his thoughts, actions, and words did not deviate from truth, this magical light would accompany him.

He must always remain vigilant.

*

Hushang closed his eyes and took a deep breath. Anahita opened her hands and the light of wisdom gently entered Hushang's body through his head, engulfing his entire being.

When Hushang opened his eyelids, Anahita had ascended to the sky on her chariot.

The young man descended from the mountain peak with the energy of a thousand strong-bodied warriors and the wisdom of hundreds of thousands of good thoughts.

From that moment, he felt a tremendous power within himself and saw himself capable of saving humans from the clutches of the savage demons.

*

While immersed in such thoughts, Hushang heard a faint rustling sound. He listened carefully to see where the sound was coming from. He felt a creature was following him. Suddenly, he saw a black snake among the rocks and remembered that harmful crawlers are soldiers of Darkness.

He thought to himself: Surely this snake is following me because of the valuable gift of Anahita, and it wants to destroy me with its venom!

The snake got closer to Hushang and stuck out its long tongue to bite him.

Hushang looked around to find a way to escape or a means to defend himself. There was nothing in the mountains except large rocks. He picked up a piece of rock and threw it at the snake[61]. At the moment the rock hit the snake, a flame ignited. The flame flickered, and there was no longer any sign of the black snake.

There was only light and more light.

Hushang looked at the flame in astonishment. This was the first time that fire had come to earth. Neither Hushang nor any human before him had ever seen fire.

Until that day, fire had only lived in the upper world of light and sky, alongside Light and angels, alongside stars, moon, sun, and on clouds. But now, because of Hushang's bravery, it had come to earth to be the companion of humans.

From that time on, and with the presence of fire in human life, everything took on a fresh color and smell. The dark nights became illuminated, and humans did not feel lonely in the darkness. It was from those days that people were able to cook their food on fire and take refuge near the warm flames to escape from the Cold-Demon.

In short, since the friendship of humans with fire, life became more beautiful and happier.

Hushang and his children also decided to celebrate this friendship, on the tenth of Bahman's month, which is the first day of the presence of fire on earth. They called this great celebration the Sadeh festival, a celebration that has been held for years throughout Persia.

After the friendship of man and fire, Hushang's popularity also increased, so much so that he was able to rule over seven lands—the whole world—as the king of truths.[62]

*

One day, the men of Persia brought themselves to the king of the seven lands and reported that Darkness had sent demons to the south of Mount Damavand.[63]

As soon as Hushang realized that people were not safe from the torment of the demons, he mounted his horse and galloped to Mount Damavand. He was on the road for one day and night.

When he reached the peak of Damavand, he looked at the foot of the mountain. Wherever he looked, he saw large black demons whose heads reached halfway up the mountain. Each of their feet was as wide as a field.

The demons were going up and down savagely, crushing people's houses under their feet, and shouting happily.

Hushang looked at the bodies of the demons and then at his own body. There was no way he could wrestle with them and have a hand-to-hand fight.

(Let's not forget that people had not yet learned the making of swords and spears from Angel Shahrivar. For this reason, Hushang had to fight hand-to-hand.)

Now was exactly the time when Hushang had to use the power of wisdom. He looked around to find a way to fight. His eyes fell on the large rocks above the mountain, and an idea came to his mind. He had the power of a thousand men and could easily lift the rocks.

So, he put the large rocks on his shoulder and pulled them up to the top of Damavand. He targeted the demons, and threw the rocks at them.

The first rock that hit the first demon attracted the attention of the demons to the top of the mountain. They saw Hushang, who with a small body, was throwing huge rocks at them.

The demons set foot on the slope of the mountain to pull Hushang from the peak to the bottom. But the slope of Damavand was covered with river water, and they slipped.

Hushang did not give the demons a chance to find a way to reach the top of the mountain, and quickly rolled the stones one after the other towards them. The stones collided with the demons, and they were thrown into the valley one by one and died.

In this way, the young hero managed to destroy two-thirds of those giant demons.

The other demons, who had seen the destruction of their friends, feared the king of truth and obeyed his command.

*

With this battle, the fame of Hushang's demon-killing spread throughout the two worlds of Light and Darkness. Every demon, fairy, and sorcerer shaped and sent to the earth from Darkness now obeyed Hushang's command. Sometimes they even served humans.

It was during those times that many demons worked on agricultural lands and took the animals to graze. I even heard that some of them cooked food for humans and drew water from wells!

*

Gradually, the children, grandchildren, and great-grandchildren of Mashya and Mashyaneh lived with the demons and fairies who recognized Hushang as their king.

Therefore, the population of various creatures on earth increased. Each had their own tastes and lived in a special way.

Hushang had to think about how to maintain the peace of the earth and organize his kingdom's affairs. He wrote laws for living in the seven lands with the help of angel Shahrivar, so that the army of Light and even the demons could live in comfort, peace, respect, and in a united country.

Wise Hushang ruled well and happily for forty years, and his children continued his style of kingship. Endless joy was not just a legend in the imagination. People had seen and felt it in their hearts!

6. Angel Mihr and Jamshid

Every day before sunrise, an angel named Mihr[64] rides his chariot across the sky of Persia. As we Persians have heard from our fathers, and they from theirs, Mihr is an angel with a heart like the bravest warriors. All Persian heroes considered him their role model for bravery and always sought his help in battles and wars.

Brave Mihr is a friend to those who strive to spread truth and goodness in the world. He becomes aware of whether someone is a supporter of Light or intends to aid the world of Darkness, just by hearing a sound from a soldier or a hero.

Angel Mihr never makes a mistake in his judgment, as he has a thousand eyes and two thousand ears, and a thousand guardian angels help him to monitor people's behavior from the sky. He is an enemy of lies and accusations. This is because these words feed the demons and increase the power of Darkness on earth.

Brave Mihr is always ready to fight with Darkness. Mihr has a silver spear and mace in his hands and shining golden armor which no weapon can penetrate. He rides a golden chariot that four white horses with luminous reins pull in the sky. The chariot, worthy of his warrior status, is prepared for the fight with Darkness. It holds a thousand golden arrows, a thousand spears, a thousand iron axes, a thousand swords, a thousand iron maces.

Mihr also built a large palace on the heights of Alborz, which has thousands of columns and is full of light. The light is created from the power of wisdom, and prevents the entry of any demon, night, cold, heat, disease, or death into the palace.

The columns of Mihr's palace remain steadfast against the attacks of the army of Darkness.

Every day, before sunrise, Mihr rides his chariot from the easternmost point of Persia to its westernmost point. He thus cleanses the path of the sun's movement from impurities so that the shining sun gives more heat and light to people, animals, and plants.

People respect the warrior Mihr, and everyone knows that if they speak an untruth or break a promise, they will incur his wrath.

*

Now our story begins where centuries ago, a kind king named Jamshid[65] ruled over the land of Persia and the world.

King Jamshid wished all the good things in the world for others. For this reason, the angels had given him many abilities. He understood the language of all plants and animals. He could listen to the sorrows of all creatures and provide comfort for them. He was always thinking about everything and everyone.

*

When he realized that all animals have a covering of fur or wool that protects them from the devil of cold, he thought to himself, why shouldn't humans have an extra skin? And he thought about making clothes for people.

He looked around and got to work.

Jamshid asked people to collect cotton bolls and shear sheep's wool in the warm season. He worked day and night until he was able to make spinning machines and teach people how to make fabric from threads and sew clothes.

Since the people loved their king very much, they accompanied him, and in a short time they all became owners of warm and beautiful clothes. But that was not the end of the story.

Time passed and Jamshid, watching the bright world again, realized that the variety of skin and wool colors in animals and the colors of bird feathers made the world beautiful and joyful.

That is, wherever color was seen, there was more joy. So Jamshid thought again, can people be deprived of this joy?

*

He first asked the plants for permission to make beautiful colors using their leaves, skins, and seeds. The plants kindly gave this permission.

King Jamshid made various colors by boiling leaves, skins, and seeds of plants in large pots. Then he dipped the threads and clothes in those colors and made people owners of colorful clothes.

*

Once upon a time, Angel Shahrivar came to earth and saw the king's efforts to create peace and comfort for his country. Shahrivar returned to the sky and asked Light to give a gift to Jamshid and his people.

Thus, Shahrivar—who was the guardian of metals as well as fire—entered Jamshid's palace and taught the king how to soften metals in the flames of fire.

Shahrivar's gift was very valuable, as people could gain this knowledge, make agricultural tools, and help increase crop yields.

*

Jamshid happily called the people to the palace. Then the Angel of Fire, who had been in Jamshid's palace since that time, taught the people to make hot furnaces for melting metals and making tools. Eventually, all families benefited from new agricultural facilities, and everyone could taste happiness and the abundance of blessings from having such a good king.

The angels were happy to see such a land and such a king. So, Angel Mihr, who witnessed Jamshid's covenant with the Light-army, expressed more pleasure than other angels.

It is no surprise to say that Darkness was not pleased with the people's happiness or the attention the angels were showing to Jamshid!

*

Jamshid ruled the earth for three hundred years. Darkness hated the spread of endless joy. Darkness shaped his hatred into a harsh and fierce winter, thousands of times more powerful than the lazy Cold-Demon, a harsh winter that was coming this time to destroy everything.

As soon as Light saw that Darkness was making a harsh winter, he informed the angels to make Jamshid aware.

Light warned that wearing warm clothes and lighting a fire alone could not save people from the dark cold, and they had to think of a solution.

Spandarmaz—the angel of the earth—accepted this responsibility and came to earth. She went to

Jamshid's palace and taught Jamshid how to build a large castle in the mountains to save people. The people took refuge in that castle. Then the sun and fire, with the help of soldier angels, could defeat the harsh dark winter.

The king took advantage of the guidance of the lady of the earth. The soldier angels, along with Jamshid's soldiers, dug the ground, and built a castle the size of a city at the foot of the Alborz mountains—a castle so big that all humans, plants, and animals fit inside it.

*

The harsh winter came to earth, and the storm began. People took refuge in the castle, and Fire— a good friend of humans—accompanied them to endure the dark cold.

The pure fire lit up the castle like daylight so that people could live underground. Anahita—the lady of the waters—made a river flow from the heart of the mountain, and Amordad protected the plants, and Bahman protected the animals to make life easier in those conditions. Angel-Wind entered the castle and kept everyone's breath warm and fresh.

On the other hand, brave Mihr—who owned vast farmlands on earth—taught Jamshid to farm in the castle.

In this way, people were able to create new joys and beauties and wait for the dark winter to be defeated.

Throughout the entire winter, Jamshid took steps in the path of righteousness. That's why the soldiers of Darkness did not approach his castle, and the demons never managed to send disease and death into the castle. However, when the harsh winter ended, and life on earth and under the sky resumed, Jamshid was no longer the same.

*

One day, the king sat on his throne, fascinated by the people's happiness. The endless joy of the people made him aware of his own goodness and he became arrogant! Suddenly, he saw himself as so knowledgeable and capable that he completely ignored the help of Light and the angels, the companionship of people, and all the beautiful things in the world.

He boasted that he had stood alone against the Darkness-army and had won! Pride and arrogance filled his mind so much that he ordered the people to praise him.[66] This selfish command was so ugly and disliked that its echo reached the palace of the warrior Mihr and echoed in Mihr's thousands of ears.

*

Mihr stared at the earth in astonishment to see the king's behavior with his own eyes. It was unbelievable. Jamshid—who had been a model of humility and loyalty—considered himself superior to others! Didn't he know that arrogance could turn him into a demon from the army of Darkness?

Mihr was so upset by the king's behavior that he immediately took the light of wisdom that was the sign of the worthiness of the true kings away from him.

Suddenly, the sky trembled, and the other angels became aware of Jamshid's thoughts, actions, and words. In an instant, all the forces and gifts of Jamshid were taken back![67]

Jamshid was alone and of course had no magical power. He realized that had lost everything he cared about. But it was too late. Shahrivar did not like him, and Mihr had taken away his light of wisdom!

*

Jamshid came to his senses. He apologized to the people, Light, and the angels for his misplaced selfishness. Truth be told, since he still had a pure heart, he was forgiven by them. However, the consequences of some mistakes are very heavy and one must wait for their repercussions. Light had told humans from the very first day that their choices would shape their destiny of defeat and victory on earth.[68]

*

With the separation of the light of wisdom[69] from Jamshid, blessing and joy left his land. So, the country suffered from famine.

Darkness liked to see this happen and sent a dragon to eliminate a piece of the world of Light.

The dragon came to earth, and Jamshid, who no longer had the magical power of the past, was defeated in battle with it. The stone-hearted dragon split Jamshid in half and took over his realm at last.[70]

*

With all these events that I have told you and with the passing of centuries from Jamshid's rule, people still know him by his good characteristics and say: "Jamshid was unparalleled in goodness!"

To tell you the truth, after Jamshid, the world never became so united and integrated again, and never again did such a good king rule over the world of Light.[71]

Notes

Chapter 1: Creation in the World of Light

---

[1] The narratives of this book are based on the ancient religion of Iran (Zoroastrianism, Mazdayasna, Mazda worship). Zoroaster is an ancient prophet of Iran. His exact birth date and life period are not precisely known, but his lifetime is estimated to be between 1000 to 1200 years before Christ.

Zoroastrians, in Middle Persian (Pahlavi) language, are called "māzdēsn" and in the ancient Iranian (Avestan) language, they are referred to as "māzdayasna-".

According to Zoroaster's teachings: anyone who has good and worthy thoughts, speech, and actions has stepped in the path of God. Also, every human being can illuminate their surroundings like a bright fire by using knowledge and wisdom. For this reason, fire has a special significance in the Mazdayasna religion, as it is a symbol of wisdom.

[2] Ahura-Mazda (God): The great Lord of Wisdom or the Superior Wise, is represented with the symbol of light and brightness. For this reason, in Zoroastrianism, fire is considered a symbol of wisdom and a purifier of impurities.

The name of Ahura-Mazda in the Pahlavi language is "ohrmazd" or "hormozd" and in the Avestan language, it is ahura.mazdā-.

[3] Angra-Mainyu (Devil): The filthy thought, the wicked wisdom that is represented with the symbol of darkness. In the Pahlavi language, it is called "ahreman" and in the Avestan language, it is angra.mainyu-

[4] In the belief of Zoroastrianism (Behdin), the world is divided into three parts: the upper world (light), the middle world (an empty space that gets filled with creations), and the lower world (darkness). In the first part of the Bundahishn, we read in the third section, "That light is the time and place of Ahura-Mazda, which is called infinite light. All awareness and goodness are timeless. Because Ahura-Mazda, time, religion, and the time of Ahura-Mazda existed (exist and will exist) ... Ahriman, in darkness, was deeply rooted in ignorance and destruction. His nature is destructive, and that darkness is a place that is called infinite darkness." (Bahar.M, Bundahishn,2011)

[5] Ahura-Mazda was not a god before he began to create. Because of his creation, he became a god, benefactor, wise, augmenter, and the caretaker of all. And his first creation was righteousness. (Bahar.M, Bundahishn, first section, eighth clause)

[6] Ahriman, due to his ignorance, was unaware of the existence of Ahura-Mazda. Then, he rose from that deep darkness to the border of the light sight. When he saw Ahura-Mazda and that intangible light, due to his destructive nature and envy, he rushed up to destroy it. (Bahar.M, Bundahishn, first section, fourth clause)

[7] In the writings of the Zoroastrian religion, Ahura-Mazda initially created a spiritual entity, then material light, then infinite time, and then from the material light, he created truth. After all these, it was time to create Amesha-Spentas or superior deities. In the new interpretation, Amesha-Spentas are considered the manifestation of Ahura-Mazda's attributes. The words "yasna", "yasht", and "yazishn" in Avestan, "ayazd", "yazd", "yazdan" and "Izad"in Persian today, have the same root and come from the meaning of "worthy of praise."

[8] Izad.

[9] "Vahištamana" or "Vahuman" (Good Thoughts and purpose) / Among his collaborators are the Moon Izad, the Goosh Izad, the Ram Izad, the Sky Izad, and the Izad of Infinite Time (Zurvan) and Finite Time (Drang-Wai). Based on the Gahan, Bahman is a symbol of Ahura-Mazda's wisdom and based on the Bundahishn, the color of this deity is white, its flower is jasmine, and its animal is a sheep.

[10] "Aša.Vahišta" or "Ardvahišt" (Best truth) / Among his collaborators are the deities of Fire Izad, Soroush Izad, Bahram Izad, and Neryosang Izad.

[11] "xšatra.Vairya–" or "Šahrēwar" (Desirable or supremacy dominion) / Among his colleagues are Khur, Mehr Izad, Sky, Good Sog Izad, Hom Izad, and Dahman-Afarin Izad... In the Gahan, Ahura-Mazda has rewarded and entrusted our manly behavior to the angel Shahrivar. (Doustkhah.J, 1994, Avesta, Yasna, Section 45, Verse 7)

• • •

[12] "Spenta.Armaiti" or "Spandarmad" (Holy devotion and humility) / Among her colleagues are Aban, Maraspand, Din, Ard Izad, and Anahita. Spand means sacred and blessing-giving. (Yasna, Section 46, Verse 12 - Yasna, Section 51, Verse 21) In the old Avesta, she is the daughter of Ahura-Mazda. (Yasna, Section 45, Verse 4) In the new Avesta, she has a thousand healing drugs. (Doustkhah.J, 1994, Avesta, Yasht, Section 1, Verse 27)

[13] "Haurvatat" or "Hordād" (perfection and wholeness) / Among her colleagues are Tir Izad, Wind (Izad Vayu), and Farvardin Izad. (Avesta, Yasna, Section 3, Verse 1 and Yasna, Section 4, Verses 1-3, Yasht 19, Verse 96)

[14] "Ameretat" or "Amurdād" (Immortality) / Dan Rashn Izad, Ashtad Izad, and Zamyad Izad are among her colleagues. In the Gahan, Khordad Izad and Amordad Izad are mentioned together.

[15] "Ahura-Mazda" or "Ormazd" / In Avesta, it is mentioned that Ahura-Mazda is the lord of all the spiritual and worldly gods, and Zarathustra is the leader of the worldly gods.

[16] Most of the gods worshipped by Persian people before Zoroaster's time are the same as angels in Zoroastrianism.

After creating angel Wai (Vayu-), Ahura-Mazda created the AmeshaSpantas. Then, he created other angels, including Rasti (Truthfulness), srōš (obedience), MaraSpanta or MantraSpanta(Ahura Mazda's sacred word symbol), nēryōsang (Angel of masculinity and messenger), Rata (Forgiveness), Rašen (Truth), Mehr or Mitra, Sleep, Wind, Dad (generosity), dadkhahi (intercession), Axšti (Peace and Reconciliation), and Afzungari (blessing),Dana (Conscience or Religion), Chisti (Knowledge)... or guardians of material creatures, such as Hovaxštra- (Sun), Mang.ha- (Moon), Vant (Star), Tištar (Rain), and Zam (Earth), and...

In Ancient Persia, each day was named the name of an angel (Izad). The first day is named after Hormazd, the only God, and the second to the seventh days are named after the Amshaspands (Bahman, Ardibehesht, Shahrivar, Sepandarmaz, Khordad, and Amardad). Except for the eighth, fifteenth, and twenty-third days, which are the attributes of Ahura-Mazda , the rest of the days are named after well-known angels, including āzar, āban, xuršid, Māh, Tir, Guš, Mehr, Srōš, Rašen, Fravardin, Bahrām, Rām, Bād, Din, Aršang, Aštad, āsman, Zamiyād, MaraSpant, and Aniran rōz.

[17] After the creation of Hormazd, he first created the Amesha-Spentas and then other angels (Izad)... The eighth is honesty Izad, the ninth is Soroush Izad, the tenth is Maraspand Izad, the eleventh is Neryosang Izad, and so on...

[18] In contemporary Persian dictionaries, the term for a demon is "dēv". This term is pronounced as "daēva-" in Avestan and "dēw" in Pahlavi. Intriguingly, the word "deiwós", which meant "God", was used in early Indo-European culture. In fact, "deiwós" was revered as the deity of the sky and daylight in this culture.

The most exhaustive list of demons in pre-Zoroastrianism and Zoroastrianism is documented in the 19th chapter of the Vendidad, a section of the Avesta, and in the 12th chapter of the Bundahishn. These chapters provide detailed accounts of the names of the demons and their roles in causing chaos in the world order. As per the 19th chapter of the Vendidad, Ahriman is deemed the "demon of demons". He is the adversary of Ahura-Mazda in the cosmic conflict between good and evil. The text also states that seven principal demons emerged to challenge the seven Amesha-Spentas, or divine beings:

1. aka-manah- opposes Bahman and causes confusion and disharmony among creatures.

2. Indra- opposes Ardibehesht and prevents creation from doing good.

3. Savoul (Sāuru-) opposes Shahrivar and promotes the kingdom of evil and oppression.

4. Nag.his (nāonhaiθya-) opposes Spandarmaz and prevents creatures from experiencing happiness or satisfaction.

5. Teriz (tairi)opposes Khordad and contaminates plants and animals with poison.

6. Zariz (zairi) opposes Amordad and produces poison.

7. Aēšma-, the demon of anger, opposes Srōš (A manifestation of Ahura-Mazda).

However, the depiction of these demons in the older and younger Avesta texts seems to differ slightly.

First appearing in the Younger Avesta are the oppositions of haurvatāt- to taršna- (thirst), and amərətāt- to šud- (hunger).

In addition to these principal demons, there are demons, such as:akataša-, the demon of denial/ būiti, the demon of idolatry / tarūmad, the demon that incites arrogance / meitouxt, the demon of false speech that brings evil thoughts /ūg, the demon that urges people to speak when they should remain silent / Zarmān, an old demon that causes bad breath / hēz, the demon of famine, drought, and scarcity / āgāš, a wild-eyed demon that blinds people and so on. These demons each play a unique role in the Zoroastrian cosmology, contributing to the complex interplay of forces that govern the universe.

[19] Ahura-Mazda confused Ahriman for three thousand years and began the physical creation. In this myth, the world is twelve thousand years old: the first three thousand years are the period of Ahura-Mazda's creation and the emergence of the army of light. The second three thousand years are a period of peace and tranquility, the third three thousand years are a period of battle with Ahriman (Devil) and his domination over the world. In the end, another three thousand years, Ahriman will be defeated.

[20] Fire in Mazdisna (Zoroastrian) is a symbol of the light of wisdom, thought, a symbol of glory or the light of Mazda. Yasna 62 praises fire. In the old Avesta (before Zarathustra), fire was the son of Ahura-Mazda, and Spandarmaz was his daughter.

[21] In ancient Iranian belief, there are two times: 1) Infinite time (Zurvan) that always exists. 2) Finite time that has been twelve thousand years and is called "time of hesitation" (Wai)... Although Zurvanism was prevalent before Mazdisna, during the Sassanid period, many considered it a sect of Zoroastrianism. Therefore, they consider Zurvan as the father of Ahura-Mazda. In the excerpts of Zadsparam and Bundahishn, Ahura-Mazda, with the help of Zurvan, brings about the finite time (Wai) of twelve thousand years, at the end of which Ahura-Mazda becomes the ruler of the entire existence. In the Zurvanism , Ahura-Mazda and Ahriman were both children of Zurvan. In this narrative, Zurvan had sacrificed for a thousand years to have a child, and for this reason, the fetus of Ahura-Mazda was formed in him, but Zurvan suddenly doubted the acceptance of the sacrifice and the fetus, and from the darkness of doubt, the fetus of Ahriman was formed. Zurvan made a pact that whichever of the children came into the world sooner, he would give the world to him. Ahriman came out early and smelled very bad. After him, Ahura-Mazda was born, who was fragrant and beautiful... Zurvan handed the world over to Ahriman, but he brought about finite time so that eventually, the world would reach Ahura-Mazda. (The oldest Zurvan tablets belong to Babylon and the 15th century BC.)

[22] In ancient writings, "time" is determined by millennia, centuries, years, seasons, months, days, and five-part and four-part sections of the day, as well as small Hasar and large Hasar. (Amouzegar.J, 2002, A simple report on chronology in ancient Iran) Also, in the ninth section of "Shāyast ne-Shāyast", the first verse states that the large Hasar is one part of the twelve parts of the day and night, and the small Hasar

is one part of the eighteen parts of the day and night. (Mazdapour.K, 1990, Shayast Ne-Shayast)

[23] The sky's word in Persian (āsmān) means stone. It is one of the Angels whose name is mentioned in Avesta. (Yasna, Section 1, Verse 16 - Yasna, Section 3, Verse 18)

[24] In the first section of Bundahishn, verse 19, it is mentioned that Ahura-Mazda created "Joy" with the help of the sky. However, in this narrative, the word "Joy" is used as the ultimate goodness and purity. Because the ultimate wisdom is also accompanied by eternal happiness.

[25] "Ahura-Mazda created the sky in the shape of an egg from melted metal and red stone, which is a diamond gem." (Bahar.M, 2011, Bundahishn, Section 1, Verse 18) Both attributes indicate the hardness and strength of the sky. In verse 32, it is also mentioned that the body of the sky was created from the body of Izad Derang-Wai.

[26] In the Avesta, Aban Yasht and Tir Yasht, it is mentioned about water and its place in ancient belief. Water has two guardian angels: one is Aban (Apem-Napat) and the other is Anahita (Ardvi-Sura Anahita).

[27] This is the unique created Cow or the first Cow (Ovagdat cow)
[28] Regarding the classification of animals, birds, and all creatures; in Bundahishn, the ninth section, and in terms of praising them, the first verse of Visparad (Avesta) can be studied.

[29] In Pahlavi language, it is Gayōmard and in Avestan language, it is Gayō.maretan-. Ahura-Mazda created humans in five parts: body, soul, psyche, mirror, and Fravashi. (Bahar.M, 2011, Bundahishn, Section 4, Verses 11 and 12)

[30] According to "Mehrdad Bahar", this narrative cannot have an Indo-European root. In the oldest stages of Indian and Iranian thought, the first human could be "Jam" (Jamshid) or Manu-, the first Human-God.

[31] Or "Harborz" or "Hara-berezaiti".
[32] The demon of death is called Astwihād, In the Pahlavi language, and in Avestan language, it's "asto.vidātav-".

[33] The soul of the cow or "Gošorun."

[34] Fifty-five types of medicinal plants sprouted.

[35] "Mašyane" "mašya" / Ahura-Mazda said to Mashya and Mashyaneh: "You are a man! You are the father and mother of the Human. I created you with the highest sound mind... Think good thoughts, speak good words, perform good deeds, and reject the devil." (Bundahishn, Section 9, Verse 102)

[36] Ahriman cast (made) the first lie (sin) into their thoughts. (Bahar.M, 2011, Bundahishn, Section 9, Verse 102)

[37] Six pairs of male and female appeared from them. All with Mashya and Mashyaneh, who were the first pair, became seven pairs. From each of them, children were born for fifty years, and they themselves died at a hundred years old. (Bundahishn, Section 9, Verse 105)

[38] From his head came lead, from his blood came bronze, from his brain came silver, from his feet came iron, from his bone came copper, from his fat came glass, from his arm came steel, and from his soul came gold. (Bundahishn, Section 9, Verse 100)

Chapter 2: The Angel of Wind

[39] In Avestan, it is called "vat-" and in Pahlavi, it is called "vāta". As stated in the ninth section, verse 113 of the Vendidad, the gender of wind is male, similar to fire, sky, and metal. However, water, earth, plants, and fish are considered female. All other creations are paired as male and female.

Chapter 3: Rain and Angel Tishtrya

[40] Tištar/ Tishtrya is the name of a star that was previously worshipped and praised in Iran. In the Gathas, there is no mention of Tishtrya, but in Tishtrya Yasht (the eighth Yasht) and Vendidad, it is mentioned. In Tishtrya Yasht, it is the lord of all stars.

[41] In the ninth Denkard, sorcerers practice the rites of Ahriman and with their actions and magic, they spread the religion of Ahriman worship on earth.

[42] apōš/ apaoša

[43] Spinǰaruš

[44] The fire on the clouds is called Vazišta. The types of fire are:

1. Berezi.Savah- (high brightness) - This fire burns in front of Ahura-Mazda.
2. Vohu.Fry āna- (the good and friendly) - This fire is present in the bodies of humans and animals.
3. Urvāzišta- (the happiest) - This fire is present in plants.
4. Vāzišta- (the most beneficial) - This fire resides in the clouds.
5. Speništa- (the holiest) - This fire is located in the family hearth. (Bundahishn, Ninth Chapter, Section 123)

[45]. Or "Frāxkard."

[46] The narration of this battle is mentioned in Tishtrya Yasht, verses 13 to 34.

[47] [46] Or "vazišta."

Chapter 4. Sleeping in the world of Light

[48] Anahita is the most important goddess in Iran. The full name of the water goddess, in the Pahlavi language, is Ardwisarā.Anāhitā and in Avestan language, it is Aredvi-Sūrā.Anāhitā, which means a river or a fountain full of water, and Anahita means transparent and without impurity. The description of her features is mentioned in the fifth Yasht of Avesta.

[49] In Pahlavi language it is **angel Atur** or **Atakhsh**, who is the guardian of fire.

[50] Būšāsp/ būšyastā.

52 In Pahlavi language, it is uš-bām and in Avestan language, it is ušah.bāma. (Avesta, tenth Yasht, verse 143)

Chapter 5: The Children of Keyumars

53 syāmak.

54 Hōšang /In the ancient Avesta, two groups of rulers in eastern Iran are mentioned: 1) The Pishdadian dynasty from Gayomard (Keyumars) to Garshasp. 2) The Kayanian dynasty from Kay Qobad to Kay Goshtasp, and then the narratives are mixed with the history of the Achaemenids.

55 The intention is to feel the need. The need for food and water.

56 He has this power because of possessing Fara (Fara, Faraneh, Khara, Khoreh) from Ahura-Mazda. However, Siamak's Fara is not of the Kiani type. Kiani Fara reaches from Faravak (Siamak's son) to Houshang, Tahmoures, Jamshid, Fereydoun, and other kings. Fara has been interpreted as glory, acquisition, brilliance, wealth, etc. In Zamayad Yasht, verses 9 to 96, we read about Fara and its praise, and there it means a powerful glow. Interestingly, we know today that anyone can receive Fara from Ahura-Mazda according to their profession, social class, and duty, and it is not only for kings and rulers. Jaleh Amouzgar in the book "Language, Culture, and Myth" has stated the types of Fara: Divine Fara, Kiani Fara, Aryan Fara, Mobedy Fara, Universal Fara. (Pp. 352-354) In Oshtad Yasht (Yasht 18) we read about Iranian Fara and in Zamayad Yasht (Yasht 19) we read about Kiani Fara. In the

● ● ●

same Yasht, it is mentioned that Ahura- Mazda, Amshaspands, and Izadan also have their own Fara.

[57] We see the name of the goddess Anahita, apart from religious and mythical writings, for the first time on the inscription of Artaxerxes II of the Achaemenid dynasty.

[58] Avesta; Fifth Yasht, verses 7, 64, 126.

[59] Avesta; Fifth Yasht, verse 120.

[60] Hushang possesses Kiani Fara.

[61] In ancient Iranian beliefs, the snake and all its species belong to the category of Khrafstras (creatures created by Ahriman). In the ninth section, verse 143, Garshasp is praised for killing a horned snake. In Menog-i Khrad, question 26, one of the conditions for accepting the repentance of sins is killing a snake. Also, in Vendidad, Fargard 14, verse 5, and Fargard 18, verse 65, some species of snakes are named, such as the fast-moving snake (Shiba), the bank snake or the dog-faced snake (which sits on the back of its body), the feathered snake, the black-tailed snake, and the short snake.

[62] Due to possessing the royal Fara.

[63] It is mentioned in the scriptures that Mount Damavand was among the Patishkhwargar mountains. In Menog-i Khrad (2000), question 61, we also read that the Pishanseh plain is at the foot of this mountain... In the narratives, Damavand and Alborz are sometimes considered the same. (Esmaeilpour, Abolghasem, 2017, Awake Springs)

• • •

Chapter 6: Angel Mihr and Jamshid

[64] In the sixth Yasht, known as "Khorshid Yasht" or "Sun Yasht", the fifth section praises the deity Mihr or Mithra. The entire tenth Yasht, which is named "Mihr Yasht", speaks about the deity Mihr.

[65] In the Yasna, specifically in the ninth section, verses four and five, the Yashts, and also in the second chapter of Vendidad, there are many references to the radiant kingship of Jam. In the Avesta and in the Menog-i Khrad questions 25 and 26, Yasna 9 verses 4 and 5, there are references to the eternity of Jam and his ability to make mortals immortal.

[66] The sins of Jamshid are considered to be eating meat, lying, arrogance, and more. However, from Yasht 19, it seems that a force from Ahriman compels him to think impure thoughts. In Indian myths, there is no mention of Jam's sin.

[67] According to verses 35, 36, and 38 of the Avesta, Zamyad Yasht, Jamshid possesses three types of "Farr". One is the divine and priestly "Farr", one is the kingly "Farr", and the other is the heroic and warrior "Farr".

[68] In the Zamyad Yasht, verses 33-34, Jamshid's sin is mentioned as uttering untruthful words. In Denkard 39:17 and the narratives of Darab Hormazdyar, Jamshid's sin is his claim to divinity. However, regarding the accusation of eating beef, in Yasna 32, there is a narrative that refutes this accusation. This is because, like a righteous Parsi, he refrains from shedding the blood of quadrupeds.

• • •

[69] The "Farr" referred to here is the kingly "Farr". It was mentioned earlier that since it was forgiven by Ahura-Mazda, it has a kind of light and wisdom.

[70] The end of Jamshid's story and his ultimate fate are narrated differently in various sources. In the Denkard and in the narrative of Tabari's history, his body is sawed in half. In the Avesta, Sepitiur, who is Jamshid's brother, assists Azi Dahaka and saws him in half. In the narrative of Dadestan-i Denig, he is torn apart by demonic people.

[71] The narrative of Jamshid's kingship is also mentioned in the Mahabharata, which is one of the ancient Indian epic poems.

References

Farsi

Most of the references of this book are translations from the ancient languages of Iran (Avestan and Pahlavi) into Farsi.

Pourdavoud, Ebrahim (1978), **Avesta I & II (Yashts translations)**, Tehran, tehran university: Academic Publisher.

Doustkhah, Jalil (1994), **Avesta (Vendidad)**, Tehran, Morvarid

Bahar, Mehrdad (2011), **Bundahishn** (4th ed.), Tehran, Tous Publisher

Fazilat, Fereidoun (2020), **3rd Denkard**, Tehran, Barsam publisher

Tafazoli, A & Amouzegar, J (2020), **5th Denkard**, Tehran, Moein

Rashed Mohasel, M.T (2010), **7th Denkard**, Tehran, Research Institute of Humanities and Cultural Studies

Tafazoli, A & Amouzegar, J (2019), **9th Denkard,** Tehran, Great Islamic Education Center

Tfazoli, A & Amouzegar, J (2000), **Menog-I Khrad (Spirit of wisdom)** (3rd ed.), Tehran, Tous Publisher

Pourdavoud, E (2012), **Visparad** (2nd ed.), Asatir Publisher

Amouzegar, Jaleh (1995), **Mythological history of Iran**, Tehran, Samt

Khodaei, Mahboubeh (2008), **Ancient culture and languages of Iran**, Parineh Publisher

Amouzegar, J (2017), **From Iran's past**, Moein Publisher

Amouzegar, J (2017), **Language, culture, myth** (5th ed), Moein

Bahar, Mehrdad (1997), **A research in Iranian mythology** (2nd ed), Agah publisher

Amouzegar, J (2002 Jun- July), **A simple report of chronology in ancient Iran**, Bokhara Magazine

Mazdapour, Katayoun (1990), **Shayast Ne-Shayast**, Tehran, Institute of Cultural Studies and Research

Yahaghi, M.J (2007), **Culture of myths and stories in Persian literature**, Farhang-e-moaser

Esmailpour, Abolghasem (2017), **Awake springs**, Hirmand

Akbari Mafakher, Arash(2014), **Persian demonology**, Bad

English references

Boyce, Mary. **A Persian Stronghold of Zoroastrianism**. 1977, Oxford.
Hinnells, John R. **Persian Mythology**. 1985, P. Bedrick Books.

More references for further reading

Bailey, H. W. **The Bundahišn**. Unpublished D. Phil. thesis. 1933, Oxford.

Bleeck, Arthur Henry. **Avesta: The Religious Books of the Parsees**. 2022, Legare Street Press

Sanjana, Darab Dastur Peshotan. **Dinkard(denkard)**. 1907

Silva, Alan Lewis. **Avesta Yashts and Vendidad of Zoroastrianism**. 2023, Lulu.com

West, E. W., trans. **Pahlavi Texts IV. Contents of the Nasks**. 1892, Oxford.

Zaehner, R.C. **Zurvan. A Zoroastrian Dilemma**. 1955, Oxford.

https://www.iranicaonline.org/